TURQUOISE DOLPHINS

A Story for School Day Rebels

LISETTE SKEET

Strategic Book Publishing and Rights Co.

Strategic Book Publishing and Rights Co., LLC
USA | Singapore
www.sbpra.net

For information about special discounts for bulk purchases, please contact Strategic Book Publishing and Rights Co., LLC Special Sales, at bookorder@sbpra.net.

ISBN: 978-1-68235-501-5

CONTENTS

PART ONE

Turquoise Dolphins

Turquoise Dolphins

For weeks, fourteen-year-old Scoot swam, surfed and sailed. When he was not in the sea or sailing over the waves, he was skateboarding, and spending long days out-of-doors, being active, had made him lithe and suntanned. He wore his hair long, and it was bleached fair, a bit dry from sunshine and salt sea spray.

Waking early on a morning in late summer, Scoot could hear gulls calling and smell briny air, in a breeze that lifted the curtains from an open window. For a few moments he lay still. On a polished chest in his neat, cream-painted room he could see a stack of new exercise books and a bundle of pens. Beside them lay his favourite handbook entitled, simply: "Sailing".

After a speedy shower, Scoot grabbed clothes and pulled them on. A loose, white tee-shirt; a pair of stonewashed jeans, torn, revealing brown legs. He shoved damp feet into blue sneakers and hung a precious shark's tooth on a strip of leather around his neck.

Scoot ran quietly to the kitchen to pack a few supplies. Shouldering a rucksack, he left the house and headed for the harbour.

* * *

Next to his surfboard and a collection of skateboards, Scoot's boat was his absolute pride and joy. He kept it sparkling clean. Pacing over a crunchy mixture of gravel and sand on the jetty, he could see

3

"The Skimmer", bobbing comfortably on the shining waves below.

There were the pure white sails all ready to be unfurled, the immaculate paintwork of golden yellow and a smart, grey life raft with white ropes, which was tucked into place on deck. Everything looked set for the adventure ahead.

Scoot concentrated, gathering together boxes full of fishing gear; buckling leather straps on his battered canvas bag containing parcels of food. He went to fill a plastic container with clean water from a tap.

Returning, he heard a soft whine. A brown dog stood there. It was one of those dogs which Nature seems to have painted all over in varying tones of one colour, with fur, nose, eyes and even toenails all coloured brown. It had a long, wiry coat, a whiskered muzzle, neat, round paws and silky ears.

The dog padded closer to Scoot, who was sorting through his possessions. It gave his elbow a wet lick.

"Hey!" He glanced up and met a hopeful gaze from two bright eyes. He saw a wag of the plumed tail. "You'll be okay," he said. "Stay here!"

Scoot untied the mooring rope and leapt on deck. As he did so, the dog, with sleek ears, jumped too, and they landed together just as a wave, stirred by a quickening breeze, took the light craft briskly away from the harbour wall.

* * *

Aboard, Scoot was busy, stowing bags inside a cabin and tightening cords and wires. He wound the mooring rope into a coil. Feeling inside his pockets, he drew out a tiny, brass compass. He brushed off some sand with his thumb and examined the dial with narrowed eyes. Then, full of confidence, he began to set sail. When he turned back to the dog, it seemed to give him an engaging grin.

"Huh …" The dog wore no collar, and the boy pulled off his own red scarf and tied it around the shaggy neck. "I guess you're my pal, for today!"

The sails billowed, filling softly with gusty wind. The strong little boat sped over the sea, cutting crisply through the waves, expertly guided by its owner, who told the brown dog, "We're gonna see turquoise dolphins!"

They stayed true to their course, and Scoot relaxed. He could smell the familiar scents of wax, oils and new varnish. Lifting a trapdoor, he descended a few steps into a tiny galley, where he lit gas which ignited with a pop and burned until the blue flame made water in a silver pan begin to bubble.

Scoot brewed a mugful of tea, added milk and sugar and went to stand on deck. A fresh wind blew his hair into strings across his cheeks and flipped up the dogs' ears. From a tin, they shared sweet-smelling shortbread.

After a fast trip out to sea, they slowed and sailed gently in calmer waters. Above, the blue sky was cloudless. Scoot could hear waves splashing against the glossy yellow sides of the boat, which creaked as ropes tautened and well cared-for timbers eased.

In these warm, shallow waters, Scoot knew there was a coral reef. A tall mast was visible ahead, with a triangular red flag atop, to warn sailors of what lay beneath. He trimmed the sails and lowered the anchor.

The brown dog was brave and funny. When Scoot dived from the side of his boat into the clear, blue and green water, it flung itself in with no hesitation. A peaceful sea turtle swam by in a leisurely way and the dog eyed it, then tried to bark, swallowing water.

Bending and ducking with the strength he had built up all summer; kicking his legs to dive deeper, Scoot could see the green turtle tearing up mouthfuls of sea grass. Fish in shoals of spectacular colour swam around the coral.

Soon, grabbing handfuls of the sodden fur on the dog's back, Scoot hitched it up to scramble back on deck, following up the rope ladder with streaming hair and water in gleaming droplets on his brown shoulders.

* * *

Scoot rubbed his head and arms briefly with a thick, white towel then, when the dog shook itself with exaggerated effort, he gave its coat a scrub, too. Suddenly, he felt very hungry. He pushed a lock of white-blonde hair out of his eyes and stamped below, barefoot, to open his rucksack and pull out some packages. He had a loaf of fresh bread, a wedge of goats' cheese, some ripe, red tomatoes and a dab of salt, saved carefully in a twist of tissue paper. The dog eagerly ate bread crusts and a chunk of ham from a tin, which they discovered with their heads side-by-side as they both peered into a narrow cupboard in the galley.

Scoot unscrewed the top from the heavy bottle of clean water, and poured some into a cup for himself, then tipped plenty more into a pan, which he set down, and watched the dog lap enthusiastically.

After their feast, the brown dog went to lie against the side of the boat, seeking shade. The heat was intense and Scoot's face flushed. He dug a bottle of sun cream out of his bags, squeezed some of the contents into his hands and smeared lots all over his forehead and cheeks.

He trod across the creaking timbers of the deck, to lean on the rail that ran around it. Absently burying the toes of one bare foot in the sleeping dog's warm fur, Scoot gazed into clear water below, seeing or imagining shapes of sea creatures, knowing the green turtle swam there.

Scoot kept a detailed diary of his voyages. In a book bound in soft hide, which lay on his bedside table at home, he noted down every memorable aspect of the seas he sailed in. His descriptions of such trips were illustrated with fine line drawings, executed with far more care than any schoolwork.

When Scoot decided it was time to turn back for shore, the wind dropped so there was barely anything to stir the sails. The boat leaned and tugged gently at its anchorage, on the surface of the sea which still glittered in bright sunshine. Scoot reduced the sail, weighed anchor and started a small motor, which sprang into life with a reassuring hum. He sat at the tiller, expertly steering with Brownie between his knees. Off they went, dashing homewards.

Scoot stared ahead, watching the sea. At the same time, he reflected on all the things he saw in and around the reef. The dog, sitting with its head under his chin, was a perfect companion. "Brownie", Scoot thought, would be a good name for such a dog. They had shared a lovely day but, to make it perfect, he wanted to watch turquoise dolphins play. Hopefully, he switched the motor off and let the boat slow down.

A shining movement caught his attention, and there they were! Three sleek and beautiful dolphins came leaping alongside the little craft. Perfectly matching one another's great, curving jumps, glistening with water, they were vigorous and wonderful.

"Look, Brownie!" Scoot was filled with excitement. He stood with one hand on the tiller and punched the air with the other.

"Hey, guys!" He yelled to the creatures. They were visible for just a few more seconds, before they were left behind as the boat's motor whirred back into life and it sped on, leaving a foaming trail in its wake.

Now, the shore came into view and a wind blew again. Again, Scoot switched off the motor. He unfurled the sails and his return to harbour was made in fine style, his hair sweeping over his face as the breeze, cooler now, sent them rushing forwards in the direction it blew. His skin was aglow from the fresh sea air and sunshine.

They stood, with the dog keeping close by Scoot's legs, lifting its head, as if enjoying their speed.

As Scoot brought his boat safely in, guiding it between others moored there, he saw two familiar figures, waiting for him on the jetty. His mother was a small figure wearing an oversized dark blue jersey. She clasped her hands over her heart when she saw her son, and Bill, his stepdad, was there, grinning from ear-to-ear.

Soon, they were all making their way along the stepping-stone path with its grass and flower borders, to the front door of their home. There, the boy hesitated and turned to look back. The brown dog sat smartly at the gate with its tail thumping the ground, watching the family and faithfully waiting.

"All day, *a dog* was the best first mate anyone ever had!" Scoot declared. He caught his mother's eye. Jane lifted her hand to brush a wisp of pale hair from her face and answered the unspoken question. *Could Brownie stay?*

"Alright then," she said. So, the dog came home too!

THE WRECK

Scoot lay spread-eagled, as if he had been pinned to the deck of his boat by the intense heat of the sun's rays. He closed his eyes, and thought about the treasure which his friend, Than promised they would find.

The boat shifted gently, safe on its mooring. The dog, Brownie, drank thirstily from a bowl under the tap on the harbour, then hopped easily across the gap between the wall and Scoot's boat. Joining him there with an air of discovery, although they had run to the seashore together, Brownie stretched across his bare stomach and relaxed, heavy, hot and dripping, panting hard from open jaws.

"Ugh, get off!" Scoot heaved himself up and they went home, where the dog ran into the garden to find Jane, and Scoot swung open the door of the refrigerator, looking for bacon.

Scoot's mother was fair like her son, but he already stood several inches taller. With smooth skin and a tanned face, she looked much younger than her thirty-four years. There was often a serious expression in her grey eyes, but she also had a ready sense of humour and in this, again, mother and son were similar.

Scoot's stepfather, Bill was keen on cooking, so Jane shopped for ingredients and handed them over to him, and it was an arrangement that worked very well. She was a teaching assistant, over-qualified for the post but she found constant testing of the children upset her, so it suited her to have a supporting role in the class-room. Jane married when she was very young, but her husband was feckless. He left Jane and Scoot, and the boy could not remember him.

Jane met Bill five years after her marriage collapsed and they were happy together at once. He was three years younger, and had to convince Jane that he really wanted a wife and a little, fair-haired son. Bill was smart each day for his job, but enjoyed the freedom of the boats and the sea whenever he found the time. A kind man, always there for Scoot, who called him "Dad", he deserved the name. He took the best care of them all.

* * *

The dog was taken to the veterinary surgery for an examination. A scanner was used but it detected no microchip, and Scoot was relieved. He could keep his new companion. Bill grumbled, just for show, but he agreed to pay for a set of injections which the vet insisted were essential, along with flea treatments and worming powders.

The vet's name was Joe. "She's a little thin," he told Scoot, feeling Brownie's ribs. "Otherwise, she's fine!"

"Oh, wait! *She?*" Scoot exclaimed. The whole family had assumed the energetic, shaggy dog was male!

"Yeah ..." Joe received a lick on the chin from Brownie. "Ugh!" He grimaced. "She's friendly, too!"

Scoot persuaded Bill they needed smart bowls and a leather col-lar before they left the surgery, which appeared to be fully equipped, also, as a pet shop.

A couple of weeks later, returning for her second injection, the dog stood patiently while she was checked again. This time, Joe hesitated. "You know what?" He felt her tummy cautiously. "I missed it, before! Sorry, she *was* lean. I think she's pregnant!"

Scoot glanced at Bill, who assumed a resigned expression. It was a bit embarrassing for Joe. "I'll help you get homes for the puppies," he offered.

However, in due course, Brownie produced just a single fat puppy which looked nothing like her! Bill nicknamed the comical bundle "Pug" but Scoot's mother took to him at once. Doting, somewhat out of her usual sensible character, she was determined to keep the puppy, and called him "Cookie".

"He's a little nut," Scoot told friends. "Mum likes him, though."

Brownie, who cared for her puppy quite lovingly at first, relinquished him when he became able to trot about independently. She attached herself firmly to Scoot again, and followed him everywhere he went.

Bill affected disinterest in both the dogs, but sometimes he was to be seen reading his paper with the tiny puppy curled up and sleeping in his lap, and he would absently scratch its round head with his fingertips.

* * *

Scoot's best friend, Than had a shock of black hair and a lively expression. A wide smile almost always lit up his handsome face. At sixteen, he was a couple of years older, but when they were free to do as they pleased, the pair were inseparable. Than was Thai. He lived with his grandfather, a tiny man who spoke just a few words of English. Granddad was always pleased to see Scoot, and would chat in his own language, which his grandson translated.

Every year, on a certain day, Granddad thought about a friend of his own, who, when they were young men, perished at sea during a fishing expedition that encountered a storm and was wrecked. Scoot's mother knew about this important date in the calendar and would bake for Granddad, then send her son with pies or cake in a compassionate gesture of sympathy.

The two friends were enthralled by the sad tale, and the description of the dark-haired Greek friend who was brave and cheerful.

He would give you a "thumbs-up" sign, Granddad remembered. It was especially exciting to know that a silver case containing three precious talismans was left there, lying somewhere within the ruined fragments of the boat.

When Than visited Scoot one evening, he held a roll of paper fastened with thin string. "Look here!" He pushed teacups to one side of the kitchen table and untied the string. The page, crisp and new, rustled out.

"Huh," said Scoot. "I thought treasure maps were all like, old?"

Than grinned. "Yeah! I copied it in the library!" They stooped over the page with their heads close together, one blonde, the other very dark.

Scoot recognised something. "That's the Eye!"

"Uh huh," Than answered. "We got to get between those rocks. We need to be two good sailors!"

* * *

The friends slung their luggage across a strip of water, to land on the deck, then they followed it, Brownie got mixed up with Scoot's legs, and he fell over. He sat still for a moment to rub his shins.

"A pity, Scoo', you like a girl!" said Than. They fought an energetic battle, until Brownie tried to rescue Scoot, pulling him by the hair, which was painful. He gave the dog a forgiving hug, sitting down to hold her on his lap for a few moments before relinquishing her to Jane, who walked to the harbour to see the boys off. Brownie had to go home because the puppy was too small to stay all day without its mother, so Jane led her away, although the dog turned her head, reproachfully looking back. Jane had a pocketful of biscuits, and the plumy tail soon wagged again.

The voyage was easy. A brisk wind sent the little boat spinning out over the sea and despite all his nonsense and chatter, Than knew how to read a map.

At last, they slowed. There were the two rocks, between which a sailboat could pass, and up ahead lay the wreck, a dark patch under the water. In the far distance, there was a bay and a blue island.

Scoot was careful to sail wide of the wreck. When he felt confident enough to drop the anchor, they could prepare to dive. In the water, they dipped down as deeply as they could, returning to the surface for air and to exchange comments about what they saw.

Than was sure their efforts would be rewarded. "We'll see something gleaming, man!"

Scoot could swim underwater without difficulty but at length he let himself rise to the surface again. He saw Than burst out of the water, with eyes alight with excitement.

"Seriously," Scoot told him. "Nothing's gleaming down there!"

"You just gotta dig deep, we keep trying, keep hunting!" Than was not about to give up, "Granddad says there's a chest under ropes and seaweed!"

There was a chest. On his next trip down, Scoot saw the mass of weed which almost covered it. He wrestled with the lid, forgetting his certainty that they would find nothing worth their efforts. Holding his breath for moments more, he dragged it open.

Than, getting air, watched for his friend to return to the surface and began to feel uneasy. He looked towards the patch of dark water that hid the wreck and the expression on his face grew serious. Suddenly, Scoot emerged with a great splash, gasping, raised one arm then plunged below again. Than had time to register the fact that his friend's face looked white beneath the tanned and freckled skin of his cheekbones, and saw he slipped under the water very fast.

Than was afraid, imagining sharks could be nearby. He struck out courageously, swam, guessed at the spot where Scoot had disappeared, and dived deeply. In near darkness, eyes wide, he peered ahead. What had dragged Scoot under like that?

He saw bare feet, kicking. Disturbed from its resting place, the chest was rocking with the swell of the seawater. Wrapped around it were swathes of rope and seaweed, which shifted and floated, and also pulled at Scoot's leg. He had become entangled.

Still holding his breath easily, praying that Scoot could do the same, Than chopped furiously at the twisted strings and plants with his diver's knife.

* * *

Grasping one another's forearms, the boys shot upwards to the surface, where they hung, treading water and panting hard. They stared at each other.

"You saved me!" Scoot gasped, when he could speak. Then, he fainted. Than cupped his friend's chin with the palm of his right hand and swam on his back, kicking hard through the choppy waves until they were flung together onto the crisp blue-grey sand of the bay. Again, Scoot opened his eyes, but he lay by Than's side until he could breathe freely. At last, he struggled into a sitting position.

Than felt shaken, and his sense of excitement had gone. "We don't need to scare ourselves so badly!"

Scoot turned on his side, wincing as the sand scraped his sore feet. For answer, he threw an object over to Than, who saw a silvery gleam and picked it up. It was the talisman case.

* * *

Scoot steered his boat neatly into its usual place in the harbour. He could see Jane and Bill, peacefully sitting in the evening sunshine outside the beach restaurant called the Shack. They waved at the two boys, with no idea there had been a drama.

"We won't tell them," Scoot decided. "You can give Granddad his case, but never say it was tough to get!"

Than was quiet as they walked up the sandy path to the house. Nearing the gate, he spoke. "It was my fault!"

"Scoot shook his head. "No. How?"

"Because of me, you got tied up." Than felt guilty. "I said, *we keep trying.*"

"Yeah," Scoot considered this logically. "I *wanted* to keep trying, when you said that. Then, you saved me! So, you can leave it."

A Blue Storm

The boys never told the adults that the day of their trip to the wreck included a dangerous dive. Recovered, they wanted to go out again and head for the blue island they saw in the distance, as they lay on the shore with the precious treasure saved from the depths of the sea.

They gathered supplies of food, water and warm clothes, which last seemed unnecessary as they prepared to leave on a brilliantly sunny morning, but Jane insisted such items were added to the luggage. She sat in the window seat reading a newspaper, until the puppy scrambled to join her, and bobbed up under her chin causing her to spill hot tea. Mildly, she said a word she would not let her son say.

"Hey Mum!" Scoot shook his head. He whistled for Brownie, who was not about to let him leave her behind anyway and rushed to his side, skidding on the kitchen floor. The dog evidently considered her duty was complete and the puppy, growing up followed Jane around.

* * *

The friends sailed until they saw the Eye, then they worked together to reduce the sail so they passed skilfully through the gap between the two tall rocks. They made for the island, which, from a distance seemed to be lying in a smooth raised curve, with a perfect semi-circle of shore, underneath a deepening blue sky. The dark shadow of the Wreck lay below, and the boat skirted it widely.

Splashing against the sides of their boat and foaming up to the beach ahead, there were rolling waves and as they stared at beautiful sulphur blue sand, sailing closer, they saw the palm trees, with blue-grey trunks and heavy fronds of deep green leaves.

The sun that shone so brightly when the trip began, was concealed behind indigo clouds now. Blowing softly at first, but gradually increasing its force, was a wind that, curiously, they could see. It whipped up pale blue sands and made shapes above the surface of the waves. The sailboat was buffeted hard. Scoot encouraged Brownie to jump down into the galley. She crouched at the top of the ladder, then easily made the leap and landed on a jacket thrown down for extra cushioning. She headed for the sleeping compartment, where she crept into the pile of sleeping bags and blankets, to curl up.

He decided to moor, hoping they could soon make their way to the shore. The motor whirred into life but the wind was powerful and together the friends battled, guided the boat as close to shore as they could, and lowered the anchor. Prudently, they waited on deck for a while, forcing themselves to be patient. Would the storm ease? Their craft was bobbing up and down on strong waves, but having sailed so far it was unthinkable to decide they dare not complete their journey with a final swim to shore!

There came a few moments of peace. The wind did ease, and the friends made a fast decision, collected the dog from below, and started to scramble down a rope ladder into a slightly calmer sea. Than went first, since Brownie had to be lowered into his arms before Scoot made his descent. She was not enthusiastic about making a leap this time, despite her determination to be a part of everything! Perhaps her instincts warned her against this adventure, but once in the water, she recovered her courage, doggy-paddled, and followed Scoot.

Only submerged up to their shoulders after all, the boys could swim, then wade out of the sea and reach their destination. There, fascinated by the colourful sand, they knelt to examine it and found it was made up of fragments of blue and turquoise seashells. They stowed a few of the most beautiful, whole shells inside rucksacks, which they carried on their backs.

Plunging amongst the trees, they felt protected from the wind, which had gathered force again. They saw great tropical blooms in the leaves, heavy vines, a snake ... Exploring, they became separated from one another.

An hour passed, and Scoot began to wonder where Than was. He called, listened then, hearing no reply, began to hunt, with Brownie closely at his heels. At length, to his relief, Scoot stumbled over Than's rucksack. Looking up, he could see his friend, clinging to the trunk of a tall palm tree.

Than suddenly received a mighty swipe on the side of the head from a branch which had been whipped by the wind. He lost his grip at once, and fell.

After a fraction of a second in startled hesitation, Scoot rushed to the patch of ground where Than lay. He bent down, then crouched, putting his hands either side of his friend's face. There was a wound above Than's right eye, but Scoot didn't think it looked deep. He was glad of the comforting presence of the dog at his side, and he removed the soft tie from her neck and used it to stem a trickle of blood.

"C'mon man," he said, anxiously. "Hey! Try to think of Grand-dad and what he might say? "

Dark lashes fluttered, and Than's eyes opened. He managed a weak grin.

"Uh, he' say, *you get up! You lazy boy ...!*"

It was a struggle to wade back to the boat, but the storm was easing and Scoot wanted the warmth of the galley for his injured friend. They made themselves cosy, with layers of sweaters and a rug around Than's shoulders, then, carrying hot drinks, they went to stand on deck, watching as the clouds of blue sand ceased whirling and the storm passed. Than drank from his steaming cup and stood at the rail that ran around the boat. Half to himself, he murmured something. "I saw ... I thought I saw ..." He stared across the water, which was still choppy and deep blue. "A young man. He gave me a thumbs-up sign!"

Scoot got goosebumps. "No one's there, Than!" He led his friend below deck again, and installed him in a bunk. Brownie shared the roll of blankets, keeping Than company while Scoot got the boat on its way back to harbour. He stood strongly at the tiller, with his hair whipped up in the breeze, and under his skilled guidance the little craft bore them safely home again.

* * *

Than and Scoot had treasure to share this time, because they had collected great blue shells with creamy-white centres. Jane was thrilled and made a row of the shells on her window sill.

The boys had to confess that Than fell from a tree, since there was no concealing a terrific bruise on his forehead. Before they went to tell Granddad, Bill insisted on driving Than to the medical centre.

A young nurse with masses of soft, brown hair drawn back into a ponytail, and luminous hazel eyes, was in charge of initial tests which included peering closely into his own eyes. She stayed nearby and held his hand, while the doctor examined him, pronounced him recovered and simply advised caution if he felt dizzy.

Than daydreamed about the nurse on their journey home, and made up poetry.

"What rhymes with *beautiful hair?*" He wanted to know.

"Always there?" supplied Bill, ignoring a heavy sigh from his son.

"She's *always there* ... " murmured Than. "What rhymes with *beautiful eyes?"*

"Idiot does!" Scoot said, rudely.

Than stared out of the window, whispering *"lovely surprise"*.

They drove on. "Weird, isn't it?" Scoot asked Bill. "They told us he was okay!"

"He's fallen in love with his saviour!" Bill knew about things like that.

"Well, that was me!" said Scoot.

Scoot's Mission

Than stayed quietly in his home for a week. Jane made a giant chicken pie, and sent it for him and his grandfather. One morning, Scoot and Jane were in the kitchen when a grinning face went slowly sideways, past the window. Than was on his skateboard!

"Scoo'! Come out!" He must have crouched down and run back, because then it happened again. He still had a yellow bruise on his forehead but he was his familiar, cheerful self.

"Don't let him try and grind!" Scoot went to change his clothes.

"Watch, Jane!" Than was irrepressible. He showed her an *ollie* as she leaned over the window-sill, holding Cookie in her arms and with Brownie, paws on the sill, beside her. The brilliant thing about Jane was, she never nagged, although they knew she wanted them to take care.

Scoot reappeared, wearing a pair of wide, white trousers and a long black tee-shirt. He pulled a sweatband over his forehead and went out to join his friend. They roared away, harshly rattling on their boards.

* * *

Scoot tolerated days in school as well as he could. At the age of seven, he was labelled "very able". However, as many naturally clever students know, being considered advanced can lead to bullying from some classmates, who become envious and unfriendly. Even tutors, finding themselves challenged by such a pupil, are occasionally too harsh.

"Gifted?" Bill pulled up a chair and sat at the table to read the letter, which Scoot had stuffed inside his school bag when a teacher handed it to him at the end of the afternoon. "Not just in one subject then?"

No, Scoot was above average in every subject.

Bill realised something and turned to Jane. "You knew!"

She did. It was behind her efforts to give her son so much freedom, trying not to nag. She was aware he disliked school. Sensible and supportive, Jane had done her best for him.

Scoot was offered an opportunity to join a special course. He had been assessed, and tutors considered he would be a good candidate for study of marine biology. The course was at university level.

Bill felt worried. "He is really far too young!"

Jane was calm. "His teachers believe he can do it, and he will have to complete an assignment first. If he's okay with that, and does it well, we'll all know how he might get on at an advanced level."

Before long, Bill considered what this would mean for Scoot and he became interested in the plan. He changed doubt for enthusiasm! He would get time off work, and he would help. Jane and her son grinned at each other. Encouraged, Scoot became focused and determined, feeling glad to be given a study topic he could enjoy.

Jane would stay at home with the dogs while the boys took a trip with Bill, who would support his son in the project. She wouldn't be lonely, she said, adding slightly inconsequentially, "I can eat what I want!"

"So, Scoo' is all clever?" Than was thinking about this. "He'll probably get us lost though! It's a pity he' a rough sailor!"

At that, Scoot went for him and there was a scuffle. Both dogs joined in, and the puppy got excited and nipped Than on the thigh.

Than abandoned the fight, to pull up the leg of his cotton shorts and examine tiny tooth-marks. He forgave Cookie. "Aah. He' just a baby!"

"He mustn't nip, though!" Jane said. Cookie hopped about at her feet, and she grabbed him, to put him outside. She was engaged in cleaning the sink and counters but she boiled a kettle full of water and set a collection of white mugs, steaming with hot tea, on the scrubbed table, along with a bowl of sugar, spoons and a jug of fresh milk. Homemade shortbread, still warm, was piled onto a folded napkin.

Bill and Scoot opened their laptop and sat together to begin planning. They were soon deeply involved in their new, shared interest, deciding where to go for the duration of the studies, the equipment they'd need, and how to set out the project.

He would create it in three parts, Scoot decided. He would write about his observations on paper during the week, then type up the notes and make a smart document on the computer, upon his return. There were some mathematical calculations.

Than was already losing interest in the details. He turned his attention to Jane's cookies and, with his mouth full, told her: "I love you, Jane!"

Accustomed to his expressions of fondness, she glanced through the kitchen window into the sunny garden. "I bet that puppy is on my papers again!" she exclaimed. "It must be his hundredth naughty thing today!"

She carried her mug outside, where books were spread out on the lawn. Cookie, partly hidden by a garden chair, was on sheets of file paper, apparently comfortable although there was a pencil sharpener under his tummy. He got a smack that was more like a pat, and pottered away while Jane settled herself in the chair and began to correct essays.

* * *

The galley in the boat was small, and very tidy. Cutlery, bound with elastic bands, was kept inside a drawer and plates were placed in a rack inside the cupboard beneath.

Each rucksack with its contents packed tightly was brought in by Than, who stowed them in a narrow sleeping area. Scoot had folded the bunks and the three guys planned to lay in their sleeping bags. "Like sardines," Bill reckoned.

Scoot had a bundle of textbooks, some blocks of file paper and a full pencil case, all of which he wrapped carefully in plastic and tucked away in the lower part of the cupboard.

As the gas burst into flame, Scoot clattered a gleaming pan onto the ring and filled it with water and some milk. Soon, bubbles formed and he poured the hot liquid into mugs, prepared already with instant coffee and sugar.

"Smells so good!" Bill took one, and went up to man the tiller.

Scoot frowned over his compass, but once again Than's granddad had advised them well and it was not long before they saw the new landmark he described. It was a group of three misshapen rocks and, to the right, a bay, where a curve of shore was covered with smooth, grey stones. Franklin gulls stood about on the rocks, blending in, with their grey, black and white plumage.

The wildlife was generally undisturbed, and proved to be unafraid and wonderful. The boys were careful to be respectful but they were excited to find they could observe gulls, lizards, snakes and other creatures at close quarters.

Scoot studied fairly privately, and the other two made that possible by taking care of their meals and the boat. They kept a fire constantly alight and sat around it to eat and talk in the evenings, sharing their thoughts, their ideas for Scoot's project and friendly laughter about Than's fascination with the young nurse who "saved" him.

Bill received his son's occasional questions about grammar and spelling, and did his best to get it right. Scoot decided to make two parts of the project about birds. They deliberated over this, since the course ahead was marine biology but he was given freedom to select wildlife to study at this stage and since they were plentiful, he chose Franklin gulls and the screech owls which called eerily in the evenings. He was vague about a third topic and said it would be revealed later. Philosophically, Bill left him to it, and knew that Scoot spent much of his time in a bay adjacent to their camp.

Than was given strict instructions not to climb trees. He explored, finding interesting shells and driftwood. Sometimes he crept quietly behind lizards, to take photographs.

Bill deserved a rest, and it was good for him to enjoy being away from offices in the bank. He got tanned and relaxed during the week. Cheerfully, he made most of their food, cooking bacon and eggs on the boat's gas rings, or baking fish with potatoes, in the centre of his vast camp fire. He built the bonfire high, making endless forays into the wooded part of their bay, to find fallen branches and logs.

Bill felt relaxed. He left his dark hair unbrushed and unruly, and he was clearly very happy. On a small but complex radio system, he could send and receive messages and that way, he made sure Jane was kept in touch with them and did not worry.

* * *

On their last day, there was a general feeling that they would be glad to return home. It would be good to see Jane and the dogs, and get back to normal life.

Than helped Bill to ensure the camp fire was extinguished. Afterwards, he walked down to the water's edge in the narrow bay, where Scoot had worked for part of each day during their week, and where he had been left quite alone, to get on with the third section of his project exactly as he chose. Wading towards Scoot, who was standing, waist-deep, in the blue-green sea, Than could see that, camera in hand, he was taking pictures of something in the waves. At first, it seemed nothing was visible above the water but, drawing nearer, Than could make out ... *fins!*

There were sharks!

"Oh, *Jesus!*" Than raced away, lifting his knees and flailing thin arms to run through the shallows, splashing. Scoot saw him, and couldn't stand, for laughing. He fell back with a splash, then struggled to a sitting position. He was surrounded by the young sharks, which he had befriended.

Bill had followed Than more slowly, but he was catching up with the situation fast! He ran to the water's edge.

"*Get out!*"

* * *

Jane was happy during the week they were away. She rose early each morning to take the dogs for a walk before breakfast and they went along the sea front, where she could watch the gulls bobbing about on the waves and fill her lungs with salty air, as Brownie and Cookie ran busily to and fro, finding and bringing items, such as driftwood and smooth stones. After returning to the house she would make tea and eat a croissant or some cereal, before leaving the dogs with biscuit treats and setting off on foot, for the school nearby.

Jane could often get a radio signal on the equipment Bill had set up in his study, to check in with the boys and catch up on their news. Once she was satisfied of their safety, she liked to spend part of the afternoon in her garden, where she grew masses of flowers, making the borders pretty although the ground was somewhat rocky.

After a strenuous time spent digging one day, she took a flask full of coffee and a bundle of towels, and returned to the beach, where she swam, sinking blissfully into cool waves as Brownie happily paddled beside her. The puppy stayed near the water's edge, contentedly wandering, snapping at imaginary things in the shallows.

A group of young children played, taking turns on an inflatable toy. When they argued, Jane looked around for their parents but no adult seemed to be nearby, except for herself. She kept an eye on them, noticing they seemed confident in the water and when the two boys splashed their way back to shore leaving a small girl in sole possession of their plastic dolphin, she seemed to be fine.

Jane swam, then waded out of the sea, with Brownie hurrying ahead once her paws touched the sandy beach, to shake her coat and follow Cookie, who, in a mad moment, rushed away. Jane laughed, but as she turned away from the dogs, she heard a shout and could see the child in the sea was waving hard and looked frantic. She had floated too far out and become afraid. Jane raised a hand to shade her eyes against the bright sun, and looked around for the boys, but they were nowhere to be seen. She would have to go to the rescue!

She dropped the warm towel she was about to wrap around her shoulders, and ran back into the waves, plunging, then swimming vigorously.

It was not difficult to cover the distance, but there was an unexpected problem when the girl, sobbing, refused to let herself be rescued. Jane held the trailing rope attached to the inflatable and looked back towards to shore. Was help there, in the form of a parent? There *was* a lady standing at the shallows.

"Is that your mum?" asked Jane.

The girl was hanging on to her dolphin. Yes, it was her mother she confirmed. "Mum can't swim!"

"Come on," encouraged Jane. "We'll go back to her."

Suddenly, Brownie's sleek head appeared alongside the two of them. The child kept one arm around her floating toy, but she reached out to pat the dog. Seizing an opportunity to make friends, Jane asked the child's name, was told it was "Annie", and introduced Brownie.

"She's a rescued dog. She was a bit thin, when we got her!"

Sure enough, diverted, Annie regained her confidence. "I'm a good swimmer!"

Jane was glad to hear it! She suggested they might swim for shore, all together. Brownie allowed Annie to hang on to her collar, and the child kicked with her legs and made good progress through the waves. She gave up the toy, which Jane towed behind them.

On the shore, Brownie was greeted by her excited puppy. She shook her coat, spraying seawater. Jane took Annie's hand and looked around for her mother. A strange thing happened. The mother did not advance with expressions of relief but stood still, called her daughter and deliberately avoided Jane's eyes.

Jane saw she was not going to be thanked. It didn't matter. She put the string from the inflatable dolphin into Annie's hand, and gave her a gentle push. "Well done, Annie! Go and tell mum, you're okay!"

For the moment, there was no rest for Jane. Cookie was scampering off towards a group of much bigger dogs and she hurried to capture him. She tucked his wriggling body under her arm and returned more slowly to her heap of possessions, with Brownie at her heels. With no listeners except the dogs, she mused, "I suppose the main thing is, Annie is safe!"

Jane spread her towel on a heap of dry sand and cast herself thankfully on top, where she drank coffee from her flask and lay in the sunshine, which was still hot as the afternoon wore on. From time-to-time she sat up, to rub sun oil on her arms, legs and cheekbones. She wondered how she would have fared with the panicking child, if Brownie had not decided to join them.

A tall, elderly lady threw an expensive toy for her dog, which looked very similar to Brownie. A deeper shade of reddish brown it had a heavier coat. Brownie casually stole the beautiful blue ball when it was slung from a special holder, and rushed back, to give it to Jane, who stood up, smiling.

"Your dog looks like a Nova Scotia Duck Tolling Retriever!" The woman had a lofty tone, but Jane was used to being mistaken for a much younger person. By the sea, suntanned and without make-up, with her unlined face and loose blonde hair she could have been in her late teens.

"Well, maybe!" Jane popped the ball into its plastic holder, and caught Brownie by the collar.

The woman eyed the dog critically: "Yes, with a dash of white and a heavier coat, she would be quite good!"

"She is a *very* good girl, anyway!" Jane replied.

* * *

In the house, there was a dish of lasagne with a crisp, brown topping keeping warm inside the oven and a jug full of ginger beer on the table. Bill, who was longing for a hot shower, headed for the bathroom but Scoot went into the garden to play with the two delighted dogs. A tall clay chiminea glowed red and made the terrace look welcoming.

Waiting for Bill, Jane mixed salad in a wooden bowl and warmed plates for their hot lasagne, receiving snippets of information about their trip as she encouraged Than to chat. He was happy and relieved to be home safely. He found the jar full of shortbread in the kitchen and crammed a chunk into his mouth, washed it down with a drink and wandered about the garden, singing.

Scoot grinned. Crouching, he added fuel to the stove. Wearing one of Bill's sweaters, dwarfed by it but nice and warm, his mother took a knife and began to cut the lasagne into generous squares. She started to laugh. "Than didn't get tipsy on homemade ginger beer, did he?"

Later, she might have described what happened that afternoon, but it proved impossible to interrupt the conversation as Bill, Scoot and Than were still so excited. She was glad they were all home safely. In the kitchen, she quietly gave the dogs some treats, saying to the very special "retriever":

"Well done, Brownie!"

TRACE

Scoot returned from the first term of his university course with three weeks of precious freedom ahead. Letters and emails to his mother and Bill were slightly worrying, since it was clear he was sure he knew more about the seas than the tutors. The painful realisation was revealed, when he referred to them as "those dopes!"

Than was there at the station, with a grin he couldn't control spread across his happy face. He was standing beside a shiny red car. He seized his friend's bags and slung them inside, then turned back, but Scoot ducked, protesting "Don't hug!" He straightened, to admire the new car and run his hands over its glossy, crimson roof.

* * *

Bill came home early from work and took the boys and Jane for lunch at the beach restaurant. They walked, with the dogs following at their heels. It was impossible for Scoot to move without Brownie; she was so pleased to see him again.

The French proprietor was delighted to welcome them. He came out from behind the counter that separated the eating area from his kitchen. He kissed Jane on both cheeks, then grasped the hands of the boys and Bill, before returning to the back of the room to fetch and bring to their table a basket of bread. The warm, plaited rolls were glazed with egg and sprinkled with sea salt. Clem placed tall glasses full of fresh lemonade on the blue tablecloth, and disappeared again inside the narrow kitchen, saying he would fry fresh sardines.

Clem had a thin gold ring in one ear, and long hair, worn in a ponytail. He was known locally for being a bit difficult. A customer who asked politely could watch him cook, but it was best not to say anything too obvious and to be respectful. If one took to the restaurant something tasty, such as focaccia with herbs or chopped chilli, there would be free wine and Clem's company too, when the restaurant was quiet.

Jane liked fresh white fish, poached simply in milk. Such plain fare caused his mild protest, but he would just about do it for her. (He liked her, because she spoke French!)

Clem was temperamental, but he was a brilliant chef and when everything went according to his satisfaction he worked quietly and very fast. Once, chatting with Bill and Jane, he revealed he had an Italian mother, and they guessed his expressive nature was inherited.

The kitchen could be seen from the restaurant. There were clean ovens, shining pans and spotless counters. All the cutlery lay inside drawers. "We do not put our knives for *showing*," the Frenchman warned interested observers, with no further explanation.

With a preference for neatness to rival Scoot's own, Clem wrote customer orders in a notebook then tore out the slips and kept each one pinned on a corkboard, making a tidy row of pages which no-one may touch. Unlike Scoot, however, he was not placid if something went wrong.

Once, Scoot and Than pinned a message on the corkboard. It read: *Free drinks with meals today!* Baffled, Clem had to take charges off a couple of bills when it was pointed out to him that there appeared to be a special offer. When he realised what the boys did, he went mad and they jumped out of a window and hared off over the beach.

Astonished diners, who were seated at an outside table, watched the scene unfold as the boys rushed into the sea and Clem, somewhat hampered by his long white apron, ran around, yelled and waved a wooden meat tenderiser in the air.

* * *

In the afternoon the boys took their surfboards to the shore. The rollers were huge but the friends were expert and confident. Their surfing was dangerous, fast and, as other people ran over the beach to join the activity it was highly competitive. Amongst the crowds, they saw a broad-shouldered man with long red curls hanging over his shoulders. Extraordinary for the risks he took, he was a demon surfer.

When they had exhausted their energies, Than and Scoot stood together to watch the mystery man who threw himself at waves like a crazy guy but swooped into shore brilliantly. They wondered if they would get a chance to meet him.

* * *

When Clem saw the red-headed stranger walk into his restaurant, a pleased smile altered his intense expression. *He* knew exactly who this was!

"It's Trace!" He strode across the floor of the Shack, to greet his old friend. "Bienvenue!"

Trace could be stirred into conversation about the seas and marine life, but on other subjects he was a man of few words. When the waves were low, he watched as Than and Scoot prepared to get into the water with their boards but declined their suggestion that he might join them, commenting simply, "not in *snappers!*"

Seated at tables outside the shack, answering a question from Scoot about his own college days, Trace was similarly brief:

"They were a long time ago, man. I don't use my brain! Not for much, anyway!"

Bill overheard this and felt worried. The guy was a romantic figure. Would Scoot think it cool to abandon study, live aimlessly with few possessions and spend most of his time in the sea and surf?

The older man could talk of the seas and the life so close to nature, that the boy loved so much. Almost the only thing Scoot wanted to do, was to be in the sea. He was happiest when he was either surfing or sailing. Trace was similar once, left his education and abandoned a career path. He was not forthcoming but the family could tell that, probably, he lived from hand-to-mouth, one day at a time.

He knew about boats, which earned the respect of the boy. Jane saw the growing interest from her son and, like Bill, she realised that having been struggling to accept his tutors, Scoot was impressed by Trace. Even Brownie and Cookie adored him. They leaned on his legs, hoping to receive treats, and it seemed he kept a supply of broken biscuits in his pockets.

One afternoon, a tiny girl like a fairy child, blonde and thin, stood at his knee and arranged shells on his jeans. Trace continued to smoke, eyes narrowed, ignoring the decorative patterns along his legs, doing nothing to disturb the child's game. He was in a world of his own. As they began to prepare to leave, Bill impulsively offered an invitation to join them for dinner and was gratified when Trace accepted politely. He removed the shells in cupped hands, returned them to the small girl, and followed the family. The child would have run along with him, but Clem came out of the restaurant to pick her up and bear her inside, riding on his shoulder, chattering.

The group made their way along sandy paths, leaving the seashore. Scoot, walking beside Trace, spotted a slight limp.

"Oh dear," Jane was struck by a thought. "There's nothing ready …"

"It's okay." Bill liked a cooking challenge. "I'll do it!"

He got icy packages out of the freezer, and raided the refrigerator for bowls of eggs, tomatoes and lettuces. The family waited in the garden and Scoot took coffee, beers and cola to the picnic table on a tray. They could hear the ping of the microwave as Bill defrosted bacon steaks, then sizzling sounds as he fried them, to be eaten along with omelettes, a side-salad and wedges of cheese.

The family chatted, and Trace became more conversational. He mentioned giving up his own ambition "because of one individual". To Bill's relief, he added that he felt regretful. It was too late to change, Trace said, and what had he got? Surfing was brilliant but it would have to end, he admitted. He already had a bad leg.

"How ...?" Scoot had to ask.

"A shark got me!"

"See?" Bill turned to Scoot, who laughed.

"Dad! There's no scar there!"

How would Scoot go on at college, where he felt different from others and annoyed with the tutors?

"It's not personal, man! They got a job to do. Get what you need, and get out!" Just like the other adults, Trace was aware Scoot had a future where he could be involved in helping the environment he so loved.

Later, Trace got up and composedly cleared the outdoor table of all their empty dishes then helped as Jane whisked through the washing-up and Bill returned to the stove outside, to stoke it up. Scoot and Than went into a tiny sitting-room where there was a television. They watched a film, ate tortilla chips, and sprawled across a sofa, with the dogs bundled adoringly on top of them.

Jane chose a book from her shelf in the study and sat at the kitchen table in lamplight, to read and finish the fruit that was her usual dessert, but Bill and Trace each took another beer and returned to the warmth of the stove in the darkening garden. Casually seated in deep basket chairs, they talked quietly.

* * *

When Jane went to say "good night", Trace got to his feet and thanked her for her hospitality. Unlike Clem with his French ways, he did not kiss Jane. Instead, he gave her a warm hug.

In bed, with a window open and a vanilla-scented candle shedding a small light beside her, Jane rested. She could hear the men's voices, although it crossed her mind that, unusually, it was mainly Trace who spoke.

After Bill finally saw their visitor to the gate he came to bed, yawning. About Trace and their conversation, he said he did not actually ask the other man many questions. Instead, he listened.

"He really opened up!" Jane was surprised.

"I think he's planning to leave," Bill told her. "Perhaps that was why he talked. He seemed to be signing off, in a way."

"Do you think he's going because Scoot's been getting so interested in his lifestyle?" Jane asked. "Is he protecting Scoot from making a mistake, perhaps?" She frowned. "Or is it simply because of his natural wanderlust?"

Trace was definitely a roamer, Bill knew. He looked at Jane, who loved her home. She was, of course, hoping that his family and his life at home meant more to Scoot than escaping, especially as he'd been offered a chance to study and work with the ocean wildlife he loved.

"Trace is an educated man, and a good one," Bill said. "He'd never try to change a family's plans. Is he being careful about his influence? Maybe. It's my guess, you're right on both counts, because he's truly a free spirit and he would have left before long, anyway."

* * *

The next day, Scoot and Than made for the beach as early they could. Was Trace around? The waves in the sea were small. "Snappers" thought Scoot, remembering their friend's contempt for poor surfing waters.

The Shack was almost deserted, with just the fair-haired little girl making her shell patterns on wooden steps whilst her father worked in his kitchen. The boys bought two bottles of cola from a vending machine.

"There's a random bit of paper on Clem's board!" Than whispered. They tried to look casual, standing near the corkboard, holding their drinks.

Clem peacefully began to wash down a counter. He glanced at the boys.

"I know about the message! It's okay!"

They looked at one another in astonishment.

"It's for …" Clem began, but Scoot had seen his name, scrawled in pencil on the scrap of lined paper, and he snatched the note from the board.

* * *

For Scoot

"Whatever you can do or dream you can, begin it.
Boldness hath genius, power, and magic in it."
Johann Wolfgang von Goethe

PART TWO

Scoot's Shark

Scoot Goes Home

Misty sat on a wooden step, at the top of the flight which led up to her father's beach restaurant and café. She could hear the clatter of crockery being stacked on shelves, and the sound of cutlery, being tipped, clean and hot, into trays. Her bare toes tapped an impatient dance on the sandy step, and she looked into the distance, away to her left. Across the shore, there was a still sea, and the day was hot and windless. The usual collection of seagulls floated peacefully.

Suddenly, a group of people appeared, looking small at first, then drawing nearer and becoming recognisable. Two excited dogs ran along beside the group.

Misty heard voices, saw familiar faces, and there was Scoot!

"Papa!" Misty alerted Clem, then she jumped up and ran over the sand. She took Scoot by the hand and he allowed himself to be led, at a run, to the Shack where Clem had emerged to greet him.

In the Shack, tables bore brightly coloured cloths and the floor-boards were sandy as always. A bottle of champagne had been placed in an ice bucket on the counter.

Clem was washing his hands under a steaming tap. He left sizzling pans to warmly greet everyone and inform them he had prepared a meal, and it was almost ready. They could smell garlic and onions, and could see sliced chicken and chorizo sausages heaped on boards on the counter. (Bill and Jane were never offended when

Clem made their choices for them, since his food was always delicious!)

"I'm almost ten, now!" Misty told the visitors importantly. She continued to cling to Scoot's hand, until Clem called her, and she was given the task of bringing warm garlic bread to the table. Dutifully, she collected the basket from the counter, and handed it to Jane, but she paused at Bill's side, to whisper something in his ear. When she skipped away, Bill grinned.

"She said, she will marry Scoot when she is sixteen!"

Jane saw her son's expression, and he shook his head, laughing, but he didn't really seem to mind. In fact, Jane reflected, her son was always prepared to listen to the little girl's French and English chatter. He wouldn't be cruel about her childish hopes.

"Misty" was a name that suited her well. She had blue-grey eyes, the soft colour of an early sea mist. Flossy fair hair stood out, like a cloud around her small face. There were no freckles on Misty's dainty nose and cheekbones, she was olive-skinned and the contrast with her English inheritance of blue eyes and fair hair was charming. Since Clem was half-French and it was his first language, Misty was able to chatter in English and French. She had some Italian too, from her grandmother, Clem's mother.

Jane and Bill watched the lively faces around them. Scoot had stuffed his long fair hair into an untidy ponytail. He was a paler than usual, thought Jane. He had visited them sometimes over the first couple of years of his college course, but she always suspected the life was not matching his hopes. With a long summer ahead, she looked forward to seeing him change, and look relaxed and suntanned again.

Than looked strong and happy. He had matured in the past two years, and his shoulders were broader. His hair, grown longer, fell in black waves over his forehead. A young woman named Antonia was at his side. She was the nurse who cared for Than when he fell and hit his head two years before. Her soft, hazel-coloured hair was loosened from the ponytail, and Jane thought she looked very beautiful, with her eyes so dark and glowing.

When Clem came to guide the family into seats and serve their hot food, Scoot found himself placed beside Antonia. She was sweet and funny, and they laughed together, but when she was diverted, he looked up and saw a stricken expression on his friend's face. Scoot stood, picked up his dinner plate, and motioned to Than to change seats with him.

"Can we swap around? I want to talk to Bill!"

Again, Jane's eyes were on her son. She liked his kind gesture. "You had to move!" She voiced the thoughts they shared.

"Yeah! Did you see the look on Than's face?"

Mission Island

Scoot wanted to return to the island where he had begun his project two years before. He had paid the bay a visit once or twice since then, and it was a place he loved. Animals and birds were there, to study. He hoped to find a new family of baby sharks to play with. He invited Than to go too, and of course, Brownie would not be left out.

The food they would take was of great importance. "Can we have shortbread?" Than wanted to know.

Jane agreed, said she would make plenty and he could help. After she stacked her bags of flour and sugar along with a foil-wrapped packet of chocolate chips on a board, and found the utensils she needed, she gave Than a knife and set him to cutting up a block of butter. Then, she showed him how to rub the pieces into flour until it looked like crumbs. He tackled each task with enthusiasm, scattering ingredients, trying hard to follow Jane's instructions. When it was time to add the chocolate, he loaded a cupful into the mixture, and another generous handful into his mouth.

Scoot made coffee for them all and sat at the corner of the table, holding his steaming mug, and frowning over his map.

In a little while, Than was supplied with a set of metal pastry cutters. Concentrating, he began to cut the sweet dough into neat shapes, while Jane turned up the temperature of her oven and

42

prepared to bake their biscuits.

Jane filled a bowl with soapy water and began to clean the work surfaces, cupping her left hand to receive crumbs and pastry trimmings, as she swept a clean cloth over the counter with her right. By accident, she knocked down a ball of silver foil, which had been rolled in Than's fingers after he shook out the chocolate, and it tempted Cookie, who snatched it up and swallowed it.

Bill got a broom and swept the floor with an eye on the dog. "Did you see what he ate?"

"It's okay! He can have some chocolate." Jane replied, carefully removing trays loaded with biscuits from the hot oven. She gave Than a clean palette knife, and he slid each piece of shortbread onto a wire rack, to cool.

"No," Bill indicated the dog. "Not Than!"

Cookie seemed unharmed by his silly snack. He drank water, found and gobbled up a sliver of uncooked dough, and ran out into the garden before Bill could catch him. Later, going across the lawn with an armful of damp clothes to peg on the washing line, Jane heard Cookie making exaggerated vomit noises. Worried, she abandoned the laundry and told Bill she would take Cookie to see Joe, the vet.

Joe felt the dog's tummy, and said there was no soreness. "I think he'll just get rid of it in the usual way!"

"Shall I give him something to make him …?"

"You could add a teaspoon of olive oil to his dinner!" Joe said, but he thought Cookie would be fine.

Jane returned to the cottage with her dog, and found Scoot and Than gathering up their rucksacks and parcels of food, making preparations to leave for the sea.

Brownie would go with Scoot. At first, Cookie tumbled behind her, but he quickly turned and ran back to Jane.

"It's just as well!" Bill remarked. "We need to keep an eye on his tummy."

* * *

In the bay, the friends guided the boat as close as possible to the shore, and moored it. They carried their belongings in bags on their shoulders as usual, and splashed through the shallows towards the sandy beach. They marched further, heading for the smaller cove, where they let their burdens fall in the centre of a collection of smooth grey rocks. Together, they turned and walked across a stretch of sand, stones and seashells, until they came to the water's edge. This was where Than stopped. He would watch Scoot, but he wasn't prepared to risk meeting a shark, no matter how tiny it was!

Scoot waded into the sea and was quickly in water up to his waist. He stood there, swinging his arms, letting his fingertips slip through the wavelets. Nothing happened. Sunshine warmed the friends' bare shoulders. Nearby, gulls paddled and drifted peacefully.

Then, the gulls flew up, flapping hard, and away into the blue sky above the bay.

"Look!" Scoot could see something and, in a moment, Than could see it too. A fin. Then another. For absolute safety, Than removed himself even further from the water's edge but he wouldn't leave his friend. He wondered if he should run into the water and drag Scoot away, but hesitated because the fins they could see were very small.

"These aren't the same ones!" called Scoot. It was just as well, thought his friend, considering how big the others must be, by now. The creatures slowed, and swam ponderously near Scoot, venturing a few feet away, then returning. They began to seem playful, and Than could tell they were very young. Nevertheless, he called out to his friend.

"If they circle, you get out!"

Than was not in the water, not even up to his ankles. A steep part of the shore dropped into the sea much more deeply; you could see it just ahead, through the clear water. The dog stayed with him. He stood on the sand, screwing up his face, partly because of the bright sun reflecting on the surface of the water, but also because he felt anxious.

"I'm naming them!" came Scoot's reply.

"They all look the same!" Than retired a further distance from the water's edge and sat down. Brownie sat nearby, also staring at Scoot and his activities in the sea.

It was some time before Scoot splashed through the shallows, to make his way onto the shore. "Here are the names! Fin, obviously. Sharky, obviously. Then, Sausage …"

Than rolled his eyes and pretended to fall over backwards into the sand. "Are you nuts?"

Scoot ignored that and went on, "and Sailor Two!"

"Sailor what?"

"One is a bit fat, that's Sausage. Sailor Two likes to swim near the surface."

"Why? If it's got to have a name, why is it Sailor Two?" Than tried to inject sarcasm into the question.

"There was one I called Sailor before, when I was doing my project. Swam near the surface of the water! You can pick them out. I can, anyway." He stared across the water and confessed, "I can't actually tell the difference between Sharky and Fin."

"And when they get big?" Than said. "If you go in there with them when they get big? Oh man! *You'll* be their idea of a nice, fat sausage!"

They returned to the broader bay adjacent to Scoot's sharks' haunt. They were in good spirits, despite Than's gruesome prediction. They built a camp fire, unrolled sleeping bags and made preparations to lay under the night sky.

Than wrapped Jane's home-made beef burgers in foil and pushed them into the bottom of the fire, where they cooked, to be eaten with bread rolls and juicy tomatoes. From a knapsack, he pulled a couple of light beers, and a bottle of clean water for Brownie.

Scoot gave the dog a burger. He broke it up and offered it, piece by piece, so it wouldn't fall into the sand. She ate her food neatly, then accepted a drink from his palm, before settling down with an air of exhaustion.

Scoot sat with his elbows on bent knees, to watch the sea. He talked about the sharks again. "Sailor Two is a bit different from Sailor One, because there's a V-shaped cut in the older one's fin!"

"Oh Scoot!" Than felt weary. "I don't even care! It's a *shark!*" Normally so light-hearted, Than was struggling with warnings he wanted to give his friend.

With worries set aside, they chatted, catching up about Scoot's days at the university, and inconsequential things too. There was so much they could do after they finished eating, and they revisited the hideaways of lizards and other creatures. Before the daylight was all gone, Scoot pulled sketchbooks and pencils from his knapsack, and began to draw the scene around them.

The following day, when he could be persuaded to leave the bay, the surface of the water was unbroken. The baby sharks had swum away, the sea looked inviting, and it was time to set sail for home.

THE OCEAN

Sea mist hung across the skyline like a visible whisper and the wavelets were hushed as they rolled gently into the shore.

Alone, Scoot boarded the gently rocking boat and set sail, calmly steering the Skimmer until he was very far out to sea. He checked the dial of his compass a few times but his intention was to make for the open seas. He had examined weather forecasts, believed the journey was safe, and felt determined to free himself of familiar places, for a day. He had even skirted the kitchen, to leave the cottage through a latched back door and let Brownie sleep on, undisturbed.

There were no islands in sight and as the hours passed, mists vanished and there was only clear sky above. The peace was almost complete, except when a gull screamed overhead or the waves, quickening, splashed against the boat's sides. Scoot sought open space, but he knew from his charts, the nearest land was the shore of Mission Island, with its pair of fascinating bays. He thought about the welcome he had been given by his family, and his friends. Clem and Misty. In an unexpected but happy surprise, another old pal had turned up too.

* * *

When Trace returned to the Shack, no one was expecting see him. He simply walked across the sand, holding a surfboard under one arm, a dusty backpack slung across his back, and with his long red hair almost to his waist. He was an arresting figure, but small Misty ran confidently to greet him, and Scoot stood on the lowest step and grinned from ear to ear.

Misty ran past Scoot and hurried up the steps to call her father, and soon Clem was clapping his old friend on the back, sharing the welcome.

* * *

Scoot was deliberately looking out for sharks. At length, he furled the sails and let the boat idle, barely moving along. He leaned on the rail of the boat, watching the waves as they splashed gently against its sides, seeing a shoal of small fishes, which quite suddenly became active and darted away. Scoot raised his head and looked further over the sea, where he saw an approaching fin, moving slowly.

He stopped chewing the bread and cheese that was his lunch, holding his breath, looking at the moving fin with a mouthful of the sandwich unfinished. As the shark neared the boat, he saw it was rolling from side to side. There was a tangled mass of junk being dragged along with it.

Scoot watched the creature, leaning over the rail of the boat to peer, frowning, at the dark shape that barely moved, just beneath the surface of the water. "Sailor?" he mused. Sailor loved to swim like that, with his back partly visible. The shark shifted, moved forward a little and Scoot caught his breath as he saw it was enormous. The long body swam a few feet but he noticed the tail moved awkwardly, the usual streamlined shape was wrong.

Scoot remembered his study of the baby sharks two years before and thought this one might be a more mature member of that group. He tried to remember if they had any distinguishing marks, thinking about the notes he made and eventually the completed project full of detail.

Studying the shadow, the fin and the odd way the shark was moving, Scoot did something he had only done before when he wrestled with Than. He overbalanced, and fell into the sea!

Now, Scoot needed to hang on to all the knowledge and common-sense he possessed. He made himself, after the first shock of hitting the water with a splash, float, upright, almost motionless. The shark turned in a slow movement, and swam towards him.

"I'll die," Scoot thought. He closed his eyes. He knew this environment, and he even recognised the shark, but he was quite sure it would bite him.

Nothing happened. Scoot opened his eyes again, and he saw the fin. There was a V-shaped nick just about one third of the way along it, and suddenly he visualised his sketches. This *was* a shark he had met before!

The creature stopped its awkward swimming just short of touching Scoot. There was a hook caught in its jaws, trailing a thick wire, and tangled in the wire was a mass of seaweed and a collection of rubbish. The shark was swimming with difficulty because it couldn't get away from the mass that was caught up and attached to its mouth.

Scoot knew what he faced, but his love of living things made him deeply compassionate. How could he communicate with this thing? It was not a playful baby like the family near the shore, but a giant animal in pain. Was there any chance at all it remembered him? Since he could not escape fast in any case and believing that, in fact, the creature's defences were wrecked by its plight, he let himself drift, gently, near and put out a hand. With his forefinger he traced the edges of the flaw in the fin. With that courageous action, could he communicate something?

"Hey, I know you! I knew you had this mark. Trust me!"

It felt as if time stood still. Nothing happened and there was no expression for Scoot to read, impossible on a shark's face! He pressed the palm of his hand on its side. "Wait!" He turned away, swam to the side of the boat and climbed the rope ladder.

Scoot moved very fast. He found his rucksack in the galley, pulled a sharp hunter's knife from inside a pocket and stuck it into a leather belt, which he buckled around his waist. Then, without giving himself any more time to think about it, he ran over the deck, dived back into the water and confronted the shark again.

Again, Scoot trod water, barely moving his arms and legs, staring at the creature and feeling shocked by its plight. With a pounding heart, he spoke words he knew the creature couldn't hear, but he had to hear them, himself.

"Your name's Sailor. *You know me!* So, let me do this!" Then, working fast but with precise care, he cut the hook from the shark's mouth. "You're not gonna kill me!" He repeated the phrase two or three times, hoping against hope that he was right. "You'll get better now and I'll see you again. I'll see you on the island!"

One more time, as if he wasn't scared enough already, Scoot had to turn his back on the shark and pray he would be allowed to swim to the rope ladder and scramble up and into his boat. He achieved it and looked down at the sea but its surface was unbroken now. Scoot had survived, and he was free to sail away, and head for home.

* * *

Than and Scoot had been firm friends ever since they were small boys and they shared many secrets. Now, this was a dilemma, for Than had a great fear of sharks and Scoot knew he couldn't confide this time. He wasn't blinkered to all the reasons for such fear!

Times were moving on, and there were other people in their lives. Than was besotted, perhaps even in love with the beautiful Antonia, and they spent their days together, although they both joined Scoot on the seashore often, and Than still loved to surf.

Scoot made his mind up: he would confide in Trace. He wouldn't burden Than, or Bill, with the details of his adventure, which could have had such a dreadful outcome!

So, on an evening when the beach was almost deserted, Scoot went out very late, making his way down to the Shack, where Clem kept the doors open while he was cleaning up. He was always prepared to bring wine or beers to a table and chat with good friends after dark. There he was, shaking out tablecloths, standing on the sandy steps with Trace sitting nearby.

Scoot went to get a bottle of cold water from the vending machine and said "Hi" to Clem, who nodded.

"Ça va?"

"Oui," responded Scoot. "Ça va bien, merci." He sat on a low stone wall, since Clem had folded the outdoor chairs and piled them inside the Shack against the counter. Clem went inside the restaurant and could be heard clattering cutlery as he piled it into the drawers.

Trace said nothing. He didn't comment on Scoot's arrival at the café, so late in the evening. He looked down at the beer bottle he held in one hand, and swirled its contents before raising it to his lips.

Because of the peaceable silence, it was easy for Scoot to begin his tale. "Something happened out there yesterday ..."

"Uh huh. I figured." The older man was quiet for a few minutes, his expression unreadable. Scoot waited. "Scoot, we're pretty similar. We act calm, but we're deep. You love those goddamned sea creatures and so do I, but a passion can make you crazy. Remember when you asked about my leg? I said a shark got me?"

"Yeah!" Scoot remembered. "A lie. Scared Bill!"

"You knew it was a wind-up. My arm, now ...." Trace raised his left arm, and pointed to a long scar which ran from his arm pit and around the shoulder. Scoot wondered how come he hadn't spotted it before, then looked at his friend's long locks of red hair. When the hair was wet from seawater, it clung across Trace's back and over his shoulders and chest. "Let's just say, I did a dumb thing."

Scoot told Trace about the shark named Sailor. He went right ahead and described the whole incident. When he came to the part where he had removed the tangled rubbish from the shark's jaws, and was faced with escaping, out of the water and back into his boat, he could barely express himself. His breath got short.

"I almost don't know what happened," Scoot confessed. "I mean, how did I get out of the sea? What made me fast enough? If I wasn't fast, was I even in danger?" Trace raised his eyebrows, but Scoot went on. "I actually hung all that junk over my shoulder, and dragged it out of the water with me! I slung it below deck; it's there, but I can't really remember how I did that!"

Trace knew about times like that. "It's the scare!" He frowned. "The shock. There's a name for it. Fugue. You'll probably never get that part back, but you don't need that memory, Scoot."

What if the shark, despite the fact it can eat now, gets infected? This was Scoot's great worry. He knew he couldn't tell Than, who was certainly courageous when he rescued Scoot from the dive for treasure, but it wasn't fair to draw him into this. Than was scared to death of sharks!

Nor Bill, who would be frantic with worry. Nor Jane. Trace knew these things. He thought about Jane's sweet, serious face as she described her efforts to raise Scoot well, and her concerns to do the right thing for her gifted son.

"I said I'd see it again," Scoot confessed.

Trace shook his head. "Shark won't care!"

"No, but I want to … and I'll go to Mission Island. Come?"

"Jesus, Scoot! That thing might not swim near there for a month!"

"Or it might go tomorrow, looking for me!"

"If it's infected and sick?"

"I don't know." Scoot shrugged. "I want to find out!"

A Challenge

Trace and Scoot sailed to the island. There, two years before, Scoot had studied and played with baby sharks, and more recently, he found a new family of sharks when he visited the bay with Than.

Trace took charge of the boat's tiller. "Chasing sharks is a serious business," he observed. The sea breeze whipped his hair across his face. He shook his head and brushed the back of his hand across his eyes. He went on. "They've got no mercy."

Scoot listened respectfully. The longing to find out if Sailor had survived was mixed, equally, with fear, but he voiced a hopeful thought. "Some wild things do trust humans."

The older man glanced at Scoot's face. "There's plenty o' men tried to tame a wild thing." He was unsmiling. "Fool thinks he did. Then, nature takes over."

Scoot took a bottle of water, went to the lower part of the shore and sat, cross-legged, silently watching the great stretch of seawater. By turns, he gazed at the movement of the waves, and the distant horizon before him.

Trace popped a beer can. He remembered Jane's concern about her son and got bread and cheese from the rucksack at his feet, cut a sandwich and took it to the boy. When minutes became hours and they waited on, he pulled his woollen hat over his eyes and fell asleep.

All day long, they lingered there on the seashore. Scoot's eyes ached from scanning the surface of the sea but it was calm, slate smooth, almost unchanging. Franklin's Gulls swam, undisturbed. Scoot had felt haunted by the memory of the damaged shark. He knew he had done his best, that it was a foolish adventure and needed to be put behind him but his thoughts hadn't moved on from the potential for suffering, if the creature had not healed.

At last, it seemed time to leave the calm waters, the peacefully swimming seabirds, and the beauty of the sinking sun in the distance. "I'm never gonna know." Sadly, Scoot began to gather up the remnants of their meal.

Then, everything changed! Birds rose, like one cloud with a milling, flapping centre. There was a shark's fin, visible above the swell and surge of grey waves. Not lazily rolling, or travelling idly, this time the shark was moving at speed, heading for the shore. There was the V-shape on its fin.

Scoot shouted and Trace stirred, saw, knew his intention and lunged for him. He caught an ankle and Scoot tripped, saved himself with outstretched hands in the sand, then struggled free and ran towards the sea. Barely submerged, waiting in the deeper water just under the shelf where the beach dropped its level, there was the long body of the great shark.

Scoot was at the water's edge in the space of a heartbeat, but it was enough time for Trace to say a mental prayer. Had his message hit home?

Trace struggled to his feet, cursing his game leg. Before him was a scene that happened and disappeared in seconds. The shark raised itself, ugly jaws opened, Scoot saw its mouth, healed and normal. Then, it was over and Sailor left, moving fast again. Far out to sea, there, for a few seconds more, was the sight of a fin in the waves. It changed direction, and was gone.

Scoot stood still. "My heart!" He put a hand to his chest. "It's going like mad!"

At his side, Trace glanced briefly at Scoot. "Good!" He turned away from the sea, and began to make his way back towards the further bay, where the boat was moored.

Scoot followed. "Good?"

"Was startin' to think you ain't natural!"

Scoot had done what he set out to do. The nagging torment of needing to know the outcome of his sea rescue was over. On the way home, the sea was grey and full of rolling waves, and the air was cold. Despite his relief, Scoot felt downcast, and he struggled with his thoughts.

"I had to save it!"

"You wanted to stop the suffering." It was a statement. Trace stared at the ocean ahead. He had pulled his knitted cap low, over his brow.

"It's like a killing machine, though!"

"Sea life. God's creatures. You didn't create them!" After a moment, Trace spoke again. "Don't know what you could have done, if it was sick."

"No," Scoot agreed. "Tell Joe, maybe?"

Trace chuckled at that. He caught Scoot's eye, and they burst into laughter, picturing the mild-mannered vet, who dealt mostly with the pampered pets of local people, being confronted with a shark.

Land was in sight when Trace asked a question. "What's the matter with your course?"

"Box-ticking," replied Scott wearily. "That's all."

"But you get to see real animals sometimes?"

"Yeah" Scoot replied. "Seals, young ones. They clicker-train them."

Trace looked serious. His expression darkened. "Ah. Mind control, instead of making a bond."

"Those tutors have done courses, but they don't know ..." Scoot broke off.

"What we know?"

"That's it! I wouldn't do it, the clicker thing, and *that* caused a big old fuss. Nobody there was … well … sensitive. It's nothing but theory, to them."

A Decision

Scoot had many thoughts after his return home from the ocean with Trace. He found he was exhausted, and that night he went to bed early, and fell into a deep sleep. When he awoke the next morning, he collected a bottle of water and a handful of cookies from the kitchen, and then returned to his room. Brownie went too, relieved to be with him. Scoot wouldn't turn her away, and despite her heavy weight across his legs, he slept again.

At last, waking at around midday, Scoot emerged from his room and went looking for Jane. He found her in the garden and cast himself down on the grass. His mother glanced at him, then turned again to her plants, while Cookie greeted Brownie riotously, and they played. Scoot had made a decision, and he didn't want to wait any longer before he told Jane about it.

Scoot would abandon the course. He had completed two full years and gained some useful qualifications, but he couldn't face returning for another year. Instead, he planned to travel. He would take his art materials, keep a diary, build on his notes and sketches and turn them into a book. For sure, he would go with Trace, perhaps for a year, but he would never let his mother worry about him. He would check in with messages and calls, and he promised to keep safe.

Jane listened. "You'll have your diploma." She frowned. "You won't get a degree."

"The thing is, Jane, I've got to *live it*!"

She nodded. "I need to talk to Bill, though."

Scoot grinned. "Yeah, I know … and I need to talk to Trace!"

* * *

"Okay." Trace had foreseen the request and he didn't argue. He agreed to the plan. "Maybe, when we're out there, I'll tell you about how I hurt my arm. Guess, probably, I should."

Bill had his concerns, as always. "Shall we take Scoot away on a long holiday? Shall we give him more time to think?"

"If Scoot needs to make a final decision, he needs to be here," Jane answered. "If he trusts us, just to listen, not take him away from Trace or to try to chase the guy away, he will keep telling us his plans, as he always does. Even if we don't say or do anything to change his mind, at least we will know what's in it." She was so sensible. Bill saw that, if Scoot was prevented from going with Trace, he might leave home all on his own, and that would be worse.

Together, Bill and Jane decided they would let Scoot make up his own mind. "Scoot is growing up. He's nearly grown, really. In the future, there'll be plenty he never tells us." Bill's words made Jane cry, but he was right and she couldn't argue.

They decided to invite Trace along to their home, to share a meal, just as they did two years before. They asked Than, Antonia and Granddad to come too, and Jane spent a long time mixing a paella, using the recipe she had managed to persuade Clem to share.

In the event, it was a lively party. With a drop of whisky inside him, Granddad was very funny; he hopped up on a chair and sang songs which they struggled to understand but found amusing nevertheless, because of the old man's quaint delivery. Than had a similar, unconscious comic genius, and he waved his own glass around and joined in with some of the verses.

They all ate vast amounts of paella, the dogs got stuffed with titbits, and Jane and Bill relaxed. They saw the friendship which had developed between their son and Trace, and the composed way in which Scoot conducted himself.

When Clem and his wife, Rachel walked up the stony pathway to the cottage, they brought Misty, who wore her father's grey sweater wrapped around her shoulders. She looked sleepy, but perked up when she saw the group, and asked to hold Cookie and sit beside Scoot, two requests which were readily granted.

Misty stroked the young dog's fuzzy head and ran her fingers over his collar which was sparkly. "Look," she told Cookie. "Your collar matches my bag!" She had a dainty handbag on a long strap over one shoulder. "The dogs' names are clever," she remarked. "A chocolate brownie and a cookie!"

"Well," said Scoot, "I just named Brownie because of her colour!"

"Who named this one?"

"Mum." He laughed. "She would have made the connection! She's always baking."

"Call the next one *Shorty*, because of Jane's shortbread?" Misty suggested.

"No more dogs!" Brownie had just walked clumsily over Bill's bare toes, and he was rubbing them.

Clem sampled the paella from a vast pan, still warm inside the oven and pronounced it "très bon!" He spooned some into dishes for himself and Rachel. After eating, Rachel linked arms with Jane and they walked about the dark garden, talking in quiet voices about their hopes for their children. Antonia listened to Misty's chatter, which was (at first) about how much she loved dogs and would have a puppy of her own one day, then moved on to the fact that she was definitely going to marry Scoot. "And it won't be so long from now!" she declared. "Because I am ten!"

Antonia looked at Scoot's profile when he turned his head, listening to Clem. He may have heard the child but she couldn't tell. She glanced at Than, who caught her eye and winked, grinning. Antonia smiled to herself, since she had a few plans of her own.

* * *

When the time to say goodbye to Scoot drew near, Misty brought a small, curly cream and yellow shell out of the tiny handbag. She had written her name inside, in careful lettering. She gave the shell to Scoot.

"My name won't rub off!" Misty told him. "I painted it on!" She insisted he was to keep it in his pocket.

Scoot accepted the gift, and disappeared for a few minutes, before re-emerging from the kitchen. He'd found his penknife and, with one of its tools, he bored a hole in the shell. He threaded it on a strip of leather, and hung it around his neck with the shark's tooth.

Jane knew this would be important to the little girl. "Scoot ..."

"It's okay, Jane!" Scoot was kind to Misty. "It's a cool present!"

Bill knew his son would not have treated the gift quite so carefully if it wasn't important to him, too. He could have left it lying with his collection of treasures from the seashore. Instead, he would wear it. Bill wondered what the future held for Scoot and Misty. For now, she was just a child and Scoot had made a big decision. He was off again!

POSTSCRIPT

When Misty was sixteen years of age, her hair was still silken and pale. It fell in loose, cobwebby fronds around her small face. Tiny beads were threaded into strands at her temples. Her eyes were blue-grey in colour; long-lashed, they held a solemn expression. She had smooth, olive skin, and she had grown tall, almost as tall as Scoot, with a hand-span waist and legs made strong from surfing.

Misty stood on the pale green carpet of her bedroom, looking through an open window at the early morning mists that hung over a distant sea. She wore a white silk slip, and her legs were bare. In her hands, she clasped her wedding bouquet. Spilling over with flowers and ferns, all white and green, it held lily of the valley, white rosebuds and Gypsophila, or *baby's breath*.

Scoot's mother, Jane brought her dress, wrapped in folds of rustling tissue. Misty was a child who had grown up by the sea; she had learned to swim, surf and sail, but she was no tomboy. She had chosen a truly beautiful wedding dress, with white and creamy lace, a long veil, a scalloped neckline and cuffs, and a dainty tiara.

How would Misty like to wear her hair? Two mothers were poised to help her make it look lovely. "Up or down?" Rachel asked.

"Not on top of my head!" Misty said.

"Loose, then?"

"No, not loose ..." Misty had considered this already. "Can we

61

pin it into a bun?"

So, Jane and Rachel combed, and brushed, and ran palms full of foaming mousse through the long fair hair, then twirled and pinned it into a shining coil on the nape of Misty's neck.

In the cottage garden, beneath a bower smothered in flowers, Scoot was standing before the registrar, waiting for his bride. Of course, it was Than who stood at his right-hand side. At twenty-two years of age, Scoot was not so different from his younger self but today he wore a suit made of pale linen, and at the lapel was a modest boutonniere, handmade with ferns and flowers by Jane. His long hair had been sleekly smoothed, drawn back, and tamed into a ponytail. He heard a gasp from the people who waited behind him, glanced around, and caught his breath.

Leaning on her father's arm, Misty walked towards Scoot. Her face was just visible beneath translucent veiling, and her dress was a froth of white lace and sparkling white satin. A tiny bridesmaid, Misty's niece, was dressed in a rose-pink shift and her light brown hair was a halo of curls. Her name was Candy. Carrying a posy of daisies and pink carnations, she followed the bride. Scoot could hear the faintest rustle of silk in Misty's full skirt, when she joined him.

The wedding ceremony was simple and brief. Than was a dutiful best man and his unruly dark hair was freshly cut but he couldn't hide his grin. His own lovely wife, Antonia, stood amongst the few guests. Trace looked unfamiliar with his red curls tied into a bunch; a white collar at his neck above his jacket. There was a heavy gold pendant hanging from a chain around his neck. His look of pride rivalled that of Bill, and also Clem.

Photographs were taken, with Jane's pretty garden flowers all around, and the bower a backdrop. Then, the bride and groom made their way along the stepping stones of the garden path, to go back to the cottage.

They were followed by the two sets of parents, along with Misty's aunt and uncle, best man Than, and Granddad too. Candy let go of the delicate bridal train, abandoning her task to skip ahead of the wedding party. In the kitchen, Jane hid for a moment or two, wiping away a few motherly tears. The two fragrant bouquets lay on the counter, and tucked inside Misty's bridal flowers was the shell she gave to Scoot when she was only ten years old.

Clem entered the kitchen, to make final preparations for the wedding breakfast. He gave Jane a kind hug. "We knew ..."

The tiny bridesmaid ran into the room and made a dive for the friendly dogs, where they waited by Jane's feet.

"Yes," Jane agreed. "Ever since she was the size of this little one, I think your Misty loved Scoot!"

* * *

For Misty

"Faith is a passionate intuition"
William Wordsworth

Lightning Source UK Ltd.
Milton Keynes UK
UKHW040459070522
402574UK00015B/429/J